A CORPORATE DILEMMA

by

Johann Webster

Published by New Generation Publishing in 2020

First Edition

ISBN

Paperback	978-1-80031-751-2
Ebook	978-1-80031-750-5

www.newgeneration-publishing.com

New Generation Publishing

Table of Contents

Chapter 1

The summer days were getting longer, and Eric felt the pain of being alone. His dear wife Gloria, whom he adored, was no longer in his life, taken by an act of heroism. His mind returned to that beach in Capri, the dazzling sun, the smell of the sea as it churned, the image of the two little boys playing in the waves. Gloria had suddenly stood up and started to run towards them.

'What's going on?' he'd called out, and she'd turned her head as she ran, and said the last words she would ever say to him.

'They're in trouble,' she'd said, they've been cut off. Can't you see?'

'Wait!' he'd shouted, but she couldn't hear him as she ran towards the waves.

The tragedy was highlighted by the coming anniversary of their marriage, and Eric knew that it would be traumatic. He had decided to drive over to the church where he had paid for a plot so that he could visit her grave and work through the gut-wrenching sadness of her loss.

After visiting the grave, he went into the church and sat in the cool interior, meditating in the peace and tranquillity. He took stock of his situation: a man approaching middle age, hair greying but still thick, his blue eyes bright and with 20/20 vision. His voice was quiet, but with a trace of regimental persona, his time in the Army was still fresh in his memory. The opportunity to get on the ladder of life in the corporate world, meeting Gilbert Stallen, the CEO of Stallen Engineering, and his appointment as Personnel manager had made for good times and bad times, comradeship, and an abiding respect for his country. Going to the church was an act of remembrance, for he still grieved deeply for the loss of his wonderful wife who had helped him readjust to civilian life.

Suddenly, a crack of thunder filled the church; Eric was startled but told himself it would pass over. Lightning lit up the nave, then again, a shattering crack of thunder made him doubt his judgement. The church became darker and Eric felt the chill of a childhood fear cross his mind. He stood up and moved towards the exit. The wind moaned through the great oak door, the storm gathering momentum.

Lifting the heavy latch, he walked quickly into the porch. The rain was pouring down, sweeping across the wide flagstones leading from the entrance. He shivered at this dramatic change of temperature and events. He decided to make a dash for his car and risk getting soaked; fortunately, the lychgate canopy was not very far and his car was just a couple of yards beyond. He ran through the curtain of water, cursing his luck, then wrenched open the door of the car and leapt into the driving seat with a single bound. He sat in the car allowing the engine to warm up and de-mist the windscreen. 'Keep your cool,' he said aloud, 'stay calm,' a mantra he used whenever something unforeseen happened.

Chapter 2

He reached for his driving gloves, the last gift that Gloria had bought for him prior to their holiday together. Moving the stick into drive, he gunned the engine, feeling the car leap forward with an instant response, his rush of adrenaline matching the increasing intensity of the storm. Wind and rain created large arcs of water, limiting his forward vision.

Switching on the headlights, he drove carefully. A sharp right-hand bend came into view. Taking his foot off the pedal, he allowed the car to slow down. As he took the curve of the road, he spotted a car slewed at an angle to the bend. Passing the vehicle, he noted that it was a black coupé, with the registration ARP 777. The plate was familiar; his boss Annalise Ridley Pollock, drove a black coupé.

Reversing slowly, he put on his hazard lights, then, lowering the passenger window, he saw a figure slumped against the steering wheel. 'I hope she's still alive,' Eric said to himself, shivering. He retrieved his anorak from the back seat of the car and, cursing the rain, he approached the black coupé. 'Please God, I hope she's not splattered all over the dash.' Eric grabbed the door handle and opened the door. His boss was moaning something unintelligible.

'Can you move your legs?' She didn't respond. Eric raised his voice, cursing his luck. She wasn't someone that he wanted to see, even in circumstances as dramatic as this. The rain was soaking him and running down the back of his neck. Spluttering, he said, 'Can you get out of the car?' Again, no response. Eric reached inside the car and grabbed her naked legs at the knees, manoeuvring them over the door sill.

'Get me out,' she said huskily, her breath revealing her smoking vice. Eric felt his hackles rise. His irritation was only suppressed by the knowledge that this woman had the power to destroy his career prospects, if she so wished. Eric obeyed sullenly, knowing that she could be concussed and badly injured. Putting an arm around her slim shoulders, she seemed fragile, with hardly any body weight. Her eyes were unfocussed, her movements un-coordinated, and her arms flopped at her sides. Eric carried her to his car, placing her in the passenger seat. Hurrying back behind the wheel, he took his mobile phone and began to punch in the emergency code. Suddenly her hand shot out and grabbed the phone from him.

'No police!' she said.

'I'm trying to get an ambulance,' said Eric, totally exasperated by her attitude. 'I think you need medical attention.'

'No!' she screamed. 'Just take me home.'

Before Eric could engage gear, she said, 'Did you get my laptop?' Eric felt the steam coming out of his ears as she insisted, 'I need it!' She spoke with the full assurance that she was in charge of the situation. Running back to her car, he retrieved her car keys and laptop and her shoes. He put them all in the boot of his car and slammed it shut.

Chapter 3

Back inside his company car, he was aware of her wet blouse clinging to her slim body, her cleavage exposed, and her skirt torn up the length of her thighs. Her unfocussed eyes were now wide open, and recognition flooded into her face. 'You,' she said, recognising that her knight in shining armour was a colleague. She attempted a weak smile and tried to cover her cleavage with some degree of modesty.

'Your lucky day,' said Eric, not feeling very charitable, particularly as the smell of cigarette smoke was now very evident on her breath. He suspected that alcohol was also coursing through her veins, at a higher level than the police would ignore. She attempted a damsel-in-distress persona, but the effect came over as manipulative.

'Please take me home,' she repeated, in a more conciliatory manner. 'I need to change into some dry clothes.'

'So do I,' replied Eric, 'my home is closer.' Her mouth opened then closed slowly; she was not used to being denied her wishes. The sight of her bare flesh and shapely body aroused a stirring in his crotch. This surprised him, as he had never felt any sexual attraction to her.

Annalise was the Head of Personnel of the biggest automotive parts provider in the UK. She'd worked there fewer years than he had and yet she had risen to starry heights and earned an unenviable reputation as someone not to be challenged in her business decisions. Also, she was not someone who understood the meaning of empathy, so he had avoided her in the months following Gloria's death.

As he drove homewards, he saw her eyelids were heavy, the warmth of the car had softened her. Eric felt a whirl of emotions tumbling round in his mind, debating whether he ought to take her to a hospital, or report the accident to the police. Subconsciously, he knew she was a bitch, red in tooth and claw, manipulating people to further her own ends. Eric felt frustrated and intimidated; he also had an overpowering desire to see more of her tantalising flesh. He blanked the thoughts from his fevered mind.

The approach to his home was a welcome sight. He sped up the short drive and stopped the car. Anna said in a little-girl voice, 'I need some help to get out of the car.' Eric picked her up like a rag doll, carrying her through the rain into the house. The warmth of her flesh added to his arousal, causing him to stumble on the door mat. Recovering his balance, he deposited Anna on the kitchen table. Then he retrieved some walking socks from a dryer and offered to put them on Anna's cold feet. She nodded sullenly, and asked to use the toilet. Eric directed her to the downstairs cloakroom.

Taking off his wet jacket, he surveyed himself in the mirror. 'What a ghastly sight,' he said to himself. He quickly removed his saturated shoes and socks, cursing his boss and the world in general, and made for the stairs. In the bathroom, he felt confused about his feelings for Anna. Touching her legs and manhandling her had affected him more than he liked to admit to himself.

Eric dressed quickly, pulling on a pair of jeans and a polo-neck sweater. Her voice came up the stairs. 'Can you give me something to wear?' Her voice was challenging and inviting all at the same time. Eric knew that some of his deceased wife's clothes would fit Anna, but he was reluctant to tell her. She appeared at the top of the stairs, naked, a small hand towel covering her crotch, her breasts jiggling, nipples erect and hard. A sly, knowing smile crossed her lips.

Chapter 4

Eric passed some clothes to Anna; she took them with no word of thanks. She turned her body and disappeared into the guest bedroom. Eric walked downstairs, feeling ashamed for allowing Anna to use his precious wife's clothing. He switched on the television in the kitchen, and vaguely heard a report of a serious traffic accident involving a cyclist and a black saloon car, seen accelerating away from the scene. The police were anxious to interview the driver of the car. Eric felt that the connection between the injured cyclist and his boss's car was irrefutable.

After switching on the coffee machine, he took two mugs and heated some milk. He heard a sound and looked around to see her, panther-like, gliding down the stairs. Her shapely legs and ankles made Eric realise that his self-imposed celibacy had left an emotional chasm in his life.

Suddenly the doorbell rang. Trepidation coursed through his body. Looking through the spy-hole in the door, he saw two police officers on the drive, their shoulders hunched against the rain. His head spun towards the stairs but there was no one. Eric released the security chain and unlocked the door.

'Police,' said the younger of the two officers, proffering his ID. Eric, though taken aback, tried to keep the panic from rising in his voice.

'Can I help you?' he said.

'We would like a word with you, sir,' said the senior officer, 'about a car accident around 4pm today, not far from here. Have you been driving this afternoon?' The steam rising from the hot metal of his car made the question rather academic, but Eric bit his tongue and said, 'Yes, I've been to a local church to see my wife's grave.'

'Which road would that be on?' asked the officer. Eric paused and then answered, 'It's the A483.'

‘Um,’ said the officer, ‘at approximately what time would that have been?’ Eric closed his eyes and said, ‘Between 5.30 and 6.00 pm.’ The younger PC was taking notes, and Eric was feeling distinctly uncomfortable and under pressure.

‘Did you see a car at the side of the road at Tatlock’s Corner?’ asked the officer.

‘Not to my recollection,’ replied Eric, ‘the rain was torrential. It took all my concentration just to keep on the road.’

‘So you didn’t pass any vehicle on your way home?’ A tone of some incredulity came into the officer’s voice.

‘No,’ replied Eric, ‘I wasn’t aware of any other vehicle.’

‘Thank you for your time,’ the senior officer replied, then turned on his heel, followed by the younger PC.

At the top of the stairs, Anna stood in one of his shirts, smiling broadly.

Chapter 5

Bravo, you were excellent,' she gushed, 'a master-class in non-committal rapport.' Eric gasped. Seeing her semi-naked, he felt himself stiffen, and a rush of blood to his head left him dizzy. Thoughts of unbridled sex and physical passion flooded his brain, until the ringing of Anna's mobile intruded. Anna went back into the bathroom, closing the door.

Feeling drained, Eric sat in the kitchen and drank his coffee. The newscaster was giving the weather forecast. Closing his eyes, Eric imagined the effect this scenario would have on a jury if he had to explain the events in a court of law.

His reverie was disturbed as his nemesis stepped into the room with obvious merriment. 'The police have just phoned to say they have found my car and want to interview me. I will expect you to give me an alibi.' Eric gasped. The audacity of the woman!

'What the pissing hell do you I think I am?' he screamed, a red mist convulsing his body. 'This charade has run its course. No way am I giving you any alibi, you got yourself into this debacle and you can effing well get yourself out!'

'But darling, you need me,' she exclaimed. 'I saw the way you looked at me - you hold all the cards, but I hold all the keys.' Eric was on the back foot, she had manipulated the situation to her own advantage.

'We could both enjoy a wonderful lifestyle if we worked together… I can unlock the door to the Boardroom while you sit in the driving seat.' Eric felt devastated that she had turned a disaster into a triumph. If he went to the police, Anna could use her power over Gilbert, the CEO, to oust him and blacken his character.

Eric let out a cynical laugh. He had seen the effect that her appearance and allure had had on Gilbert, and observed her charisma at work on others at management meetings.

She had been the office junior when the young Gilbert graduated from university, and they'd had a lusty three months in the summer of '86. Local speculation was that she would become pregnant and leave his family holding the baby. A family conference followed, and Gilbert was packed off to the USA.

Some time later, he met his wife, Sally-Ann, at a political rally. It was Sally-Anne who got pregnant, and they got married in a rush, however the child was stillborn, and Sally-Ann seemed to go into a decline soon after they came to England.

Gilbert's rekindled relationship with Anna became common knowledge again, and Sally-Ann returned to her family in America, making infrequent trips back to England.

Chapter 6

'You must think I'm a total idiot,' Eric said loudly. 'I'd rather drown myself in a bath of acid.'

Anna moved towards him, but her balance became uncertain and she caught the edge of a chair. Her body fell against him and he reached out to steady her. As he grabbed at her waist, the feel of her flesh was warm and inviting. Her arms clung round his neck, and she pulled his face down towards hers and kissed him savagely, her tongue penetrating his dry mouth. Caught off-balance, physically and emotionally, Eric's penis responded. Anna thrust her pelvis into him, writhing and moaning seductively. Her hand found and squeezed his cock, and the rush of blood and emotion overcame all his restraint. Eric felt a whirl of passion and lust cascade into his very core. Anna unfastened his belt and unzipped his flies, her hands manipulating and caressing. With the shirt falling open, and her pert breasts and pubic hair visible, Eric was lost to all reason, all he knew was a passion and thirst to possess her body.

His penetration was total and she pulled him to herself, grinding her hips and wrapping her body and legs around him. The vortex of emotion had overcome his self-restraint, he allowed himself to be engulfed by her passion. Her arms embraced him, her mouth hungrily kissing his in a fever of abandonment. Grasping her buttocks and yielding flesh, they fell to the floor, giving fresh impetus to his loss of restraint, his sweat and her scent mingling and intoxicating. Anna became more demanding and frenetic; he sensed her orgasmic tension, her body and muscles squeezing and pulling at his penis, then he heard her scream like a frenzied siren. Eric sensed his own orgasm reaching deliverance. The ejaculation was prolonged and mind-blowing, never before had he felt the agony and ecstasy of unpremeditated sexual gratification. Anna laughed gloriously. The irony of the situation was not lost on Eric, his but his fevered mind was still caught up in the maelstrom of emotions released by such unbridled passion.

Lying on his back, his breath still coming heavily, Eric was aware of Anna straddling his torso, her thigh muscles strong and unyielding. Eric felt completely satiated and exhilarated, the waves of pleasure ebbing and flowing. He knew guilt would soon override the exultation he felt at this release of sexual tension, but he quashed the unwelcome thought and luxuriated in the sensual pleasure of pure, animal indulgence. Anna seemed relaxed and euphoric, extracting all manner of physical and emotional energy from the experience. She drew the loose shirt over her shoulders and gathered it around her. She leaned towards him and placed a lingering kiss on his burning lips, and then got up and made her way to the bathroom to fix her contact lenses.

Slowly the sensation of an encircling danger, of a relationship that could go nowhere, had Eric groaning inwardly at his stupidity. He knew that he had to find a way to protect his integrity and personal freedom. He needed proof that Anna had been at his home, and while she was upstairs, Eric retrieved a video camera from a drawer.

Chapter 7

Placing the video recorder on a small table at the far end of the wide landing, he made sure that it focused on a mirror adjacent to the bathroom door, and carefully arranged some objects around the camera to conceal it. Anna eventually emerged from the bathroom, squinting and cursing under her breath. Eric watched her progress, wondering if the possibility of her falling down the stairs was only a ghoulish fantasy.

'What happened that you came off the road?' asked Eric, in as calm a manner as he could construct. Anna ignored the question. Eric repeated it with more emphasis. Her eyes had a coldness which made him regret the impulse. 'I need a ciggy,' was her reply. 'I don't use cigarettes,' said Eric with some venom creeping into his voice. 'Lighten up,' barked Anna, 'it's my arse on the line, not yours.' Then her voice rose, strident and slightly hysterical: 'I want to go now, I need to change into some of my own clothes and be available for the police when they call.'

The wipers sweeping slowly back and forth, Eric drove in silence, churning over the events of the last few hours, not sure if his experiences were part of reality or some fantastical dream. Anna seemed detached, lost in her innermost thoughts. Suddenly, without warning, she snapped, 'Stop the car!' Eric stamped hard on the brakes with a squeal of tyres and a smell of hot rubber. Anna leapt out of the car.

Eric watched her run down a footpath between two houses. Eric waited. After five minutes, he switched off the engine, locked the car, and followed where she had disappeared down the footpath. It led to a development of exclusive townhouses. Eric knew that Anna had recently got a company loan to buy her new home. Looking left and right, Eric scanned the properties, but found no sign of Anna. 'The bitch,' he growled, 'she legged it and didn't even say thanks.'

On his return to the car, just as he reached the end of the path, a liveried police vehicle drove slowly past, checking his number plate. Eric stopped dead in his tracks, anxious not to have any further stressful confrontations with authority figures. He dropped down, pretending to fasten his shoelace. He said a fervent prayer that he wouldn't meet a police car, or a woman in distress on the drive home.

Back at the house, he replayed in his mind what had occurred in the few hours since he had left the church: his succumbing to temptation, the false charms of his nemesis, and her overt sexuality. Suddenly his mobile rang. The caller's number seemed familiar.

'Hello! It's only me,' her voice almost caressing in its familiarity. 'I'm back in the office.'

Eric was stunned. 'How come?' he asked.

'I hailed a taxi after changing my clothes.' She gave a chuckle as though she knew that he was squirming with fury at the way she had jumped from his car. 'I'll speak to you tomorrow.' Then she hung up.

Chapter 8

As he sat in his den, churning over how he was going to repay her for the crass and devious way she had treated him, he was reminded of Gloria and her soothing words and caresses to his temple, saying, 'Don't worry, tomorrow is another day.'

Later in bed, he was restless, his brain was in turmoil, desperate to recover his self-esteem and not feel that he had let Gloria down. Waking early, he got dressed and went downstairs, glad to notice through the windows that, though the wind was strong, the rain had stopped. The early news channel was showing a picket line outside the automotive factory where he worked. Eric recognised some familiar faces but decided he'd had just about enough stress for the moment. Making himself an omelette with some toast and a big pot of coffee, he settled down to a nice leisurely morning. 'No work for me today,' he said to the television screen, a warm feeling of relief washing over him as the food settled his stomach.

Checking his diary, he saw that he was due for a dental appointment. Phoning the surgery, he was told that he could take a cancellation that day. The hygienist was a bubbly, buxom blonde, with an intoxicating charisma which enveloped Eric. Her seductive voice was smooth and inviting.

'How are we feeling today?' she said, with innuendo creeping into her voice, he was sure.

'I'm fine,' said Eric not quite in control of his vocal chords.

'I'm Sheila,' she said brightly, 'can I call you Eric?'

'Of course,' he replied.

'Good, then I'll get started.'

Her closeness and her wonderful perfume made any discomfort in the surgical chair bearable. Eric felt a tremor of excitement, then the conversation turned to leisure pursuits.

'Line dancing is one of my passions,' said Sheila, 'I try

to go twice a week.' She named some venues and dates and told him he would be very welcome to accompany her. Eric left the surgery with a spring in his step. He felt rejuvenated by the experience of meeting Sheila, the hygienist; it was as if the events of the morning had unlocked his libido.

Later, he phoned his solicitor, Brian, outlining his dilemma. 'I need to know where I stand if this ever gets to court.'

'You need to give a full and frank statement,' advised Brian. 'Come to my office prior to going to the police, and we can discuss what approach you are going to take.'

Two hours later, he read out his statement at the police station. It was recorded and he signed a copy.

*

When he passed the company entrance on his way back home, he saw the media was out in force. Anoraked and windswept bodies stood around, long lenses dangling from their necks, hands dug deep into pockets as they waited for the shit to hit the fan.

His mobile alerted him to a notification that an emergency meeting was to be held at a hotel some distance from the town, where his attendance was required.

Eric recognised a number of local Union officials there, including a National Union Convenor who had been involved in bitter confrontations within the motor industry over the years. This was a meeting likely to have all the ingredients for a bruising encounter which the media would relish. Gilbert Stallen, the CEO, looked unperturbed, arrogant even, and was flanked by the company secretary and several Board members.

Stallen opened the meeting by saying, 'My statement to the press was totally accurate. If work does not re-start tomorrow morning, I will put the company into receivership.'

On cue, Anna strode into the room, and seated herself next to Gilbert. A lot of huffing and puffing broke out, but

Anna's icy stare and Gilbert's aloofness left everyone in no doubt that the die had been cast. One Union official, who had taken to being rather personal about Anna's role in company policy, was told rather baldly to 'Shut the fuck up.'

Anna's remark caused a gasp from the Board members and the press. She did not apologise however and stood up to face her audience. She announced that, pending satisfactory negotiations, and a resumption of work, she had been invited to join the Board of Directors. A wave of unconcealed ribaldry broke out. Anna let a sly smile cross her lips, and with a sarcastic comment about male chauvinism, she reminded those paying attention that the company followed a clear policy of equal opportunity, for both male and female employees. She went on to reiterate that if no agreement between management and the workforce was reached by the end of the day, there would be no alternative but to proceed with closure of the company.

The Union response was incredulity, followed by some catcalls and empty threats. Anna sat down and had a quick word with Gilbert and the Company Secretary, then the three of them left their seats and vacated the room.

Shortly afterwards, the meeting broke up; some retreated to the bar, but Eric was eager to distance himself from any recriminations or rabble-rousing.

Chapter 9

Driving home in the dusk, he speculated on what the chances were of some agreement taking place by the following day. As he let himself in, he pulled the evening paper from the letter box and poured himself a whisky before stepping out onto the patio at the back of the house. The slow sun was casting a watery sheen over the garden.

Eric felt at peace out here, even more so when he was in the little summer-house that Gloria had bought him on their fifth wedding anniversary. This was his refuge when the pressures of life seemed overwhelming. Reading the evening paper, his attention was drawn to a small paragraph. It reported that the cyclist involved in the accident that had happened the previous day, had tragically died on the operating table from severe head injuries. Eric's blood ran cold, ice formed in his veins, the whisky caught in his throat. It made him splutter and cough, spilling his drink onto his lap. 'This is effing terrible,' he said out loud. Sitting up rigidly on the edge of his chair, he ran the scenario through his mind. Suddenly, he remembered the video recorder.

'How could I forget?' he cried. He quickly retrieved the video camera, hoping that the equipment was still working. Checking the display, Eric was relieved to see that the image of Anna, even in her half-naked state, was quite clear. After removing the cassette from the camera, he deposited it in a secret drawer that had been brought to his attention by the vendor of the hallstand many years ago.

*

The following day, he arrived at work early, hoping that any industrial mayhem would not have kicked off before he got to his desk. Checking his mails, he discovered a message from Anna saying that she desired a meeting with him. Eric was a bit apprehensive, as he was well aware that pleasantries were not the order of the day where his boss was concerned.

Striding down the corridor to Anna's office, he found the door was ajar and so he walked straight in. Her icy glare said it all, and Eric was half-expecting a vase or ashtray to come crashing his way.

'Why did you go to the police?' she demanded, almost shrieking with fury. 'And what gave you the right to implicate me in the cyclist's accident?' Eric denied having said anything regarding the cyclist. He reminded her that a witness had stated categorically having seen a black coupé leaving the scene of the accident, being driven erratically. Eric felt that he had said enough and asked if she had anything else to tell him. Her blank stare reflected her mindset, and her reply was a steely 'Like what?'

Eric turned and made for the door. Anna didn't speak or move but her silence said it all. Feeling very relieved, Eric went back to his desk.

The hours slowly ground around the clock, and Eric felt a cold ring of isolation encircle him. 'People can be very cruel. If I hadn't driven on that fateful road or visited Gloria, things could have been more pleasant,' he thought.

*

He arrived home and cooked a pasta meal, still churning over the day's events in his mind. Glancing at the local paper, he saw an article on the entertainment pages. It was about a play that was being staged by a well-known amateur group at a town some distance away. A Ray Cooney farce, called 'Funny Money,' one of Gloria's and his favourite comedies. Eric contacted the box office and was assured that there were seats available in all areas. Not wanting to use his car, he phoned for a taxi to take him to the station.

A short taxi ride later, he felt more relaxed; the train was in the station and an unoccupied carriage was within reach, a good feeling came into his psyche. The carriage was comfortable, and the rhythmic motion made him yearn for an age when life was simpler.

The journey was uneventful. He exited the carriage and made his way to street level. Walking quickly, he went into a family-friendly hotel, and ordered a drink.

Chapter 10

After his drink, it was only a short walk to the theatre, then, finding a good seat, he watched the curtain rise. The players were very enthusiastic and gave the audience a great boost. It brought back memories of his life with Gloria, and her fascination with all things theatrical. Eric was thrilled at the performance, and the tears ran down his face. When the curtain finally came down, the atmosphere was electric, and every face bore a wide smile.

Conscious that his train would be arriving in about half an hour, Eric made his way back to the station platform. Seeing the waiting room was open, he moved to the vending machine and fed some coins into the slot. He pressed the button for hot chocolate and was pleasantly surprised that it did taste of chocolate.

A couple of older women occupied the waiting room, and he couldn't help overhearing their conversation. He was intrigued and curious. The conversation revolved around the daughter of one of the women. Apparently, she had a friend with a prestigious job, and she enjoyed being on the party circuit. The older of the two women said that her daughter, Debbie, was in awe of her highly paid colleague, and tried to copy the lifestyle of her friend, but had got into debt and was drinking to excess. 'I think this so-called friend is a bad influence on Debbie,' said the older woman.

Eric felt that fate was playing tricks on him: maybe, just maybe, the women were talking about Anna. Staring hard at the women, Eric felt that one of them was familiar to him; the woman turned and smiled at him. Looking at his watch, he rose and left the café. As he waited on the platform, the woman passed by and smiled again.

As he relaxed in the train carriage and started to doze, his mobile chimed a familiar greeting; the caller's voice was urgent.

'We need to talk.' Gilbert Stallen's voice penetrated

Eric's psyche like no other. 'Where are you?' he asked rather brusquely.

'I'm on the train home,' said Eric, 'what's the problem?'

'My chauffer will meet you at the next station,' said Gilbert without much ceremony.

As he passed through the ticket barrier, Eric noticed the Bentley gleaming outside in the semi-darkness. The rear passenger door was opened for him, and Eric was given a quick salute. 'A cold night,' said the chauffeur. The inside of the car was comfortably warm, and a button opened the cocktail cabinet. 'Help yourself,' said the driver. Eric poured a large Cognac and sank back into the relaxing leather seat.

The ride to his boss's home was wonderfully smooth, and Eric luxuriated for a while in this pampered lifestyle. As they approached the mansion, Eric was taken aback at its sheer size. The electrically operated entrance gates swung open, and the Bentley swept around the crescent-shaped gravel drive, and stopped before the tall, ornate doors of the main entrance. 'This is some pad!' he heard himself say.

As he alighted from the limousine, the mansion doors opened discreetly, and Eric was directed into the entrance hall. Crystal chandeliers were dotted around the entrance hall, and above the ornate, curved bannister which flanked the staircase. The magnificence of the property left Eric speechless.

A side door opened, and Gilbert Stallen appeared, beckoning him forward into a panelled and comfortable ante-room. Eric was awed by the luxury, the ambience, and the overriding smell of privilege and power. Gilbert flicked a switch and a cabinet opened to reveal a brilliance of crystal and highly-polished mirrors. 'Can I tempt you with some refreshment?' said Gilbert, his old-boy charm oozing from him like cloud of incense. Recovering his composure, Eric saw a bottle of Old Pulteney. 'I'd love to try your single malt.'

Gilbert, looking very debonair in his smoking jacket and his neatly coiffured hair, poured out a generous measure and enquired, 'Would you like anything with it?' Eric shook his head.

'No, just as it comes.' As he savoured the whisky, he heard Gilbert cough a little nervously.

'I would like you to be one of the first to know that that the sale of Stallen Engineering is nearly completed, and I wondered if you had any plans for the future?'

Chapter 11

Although he had been half-expecting a major change within the company, this revelation hit Eric like an Exocet missile.

'What did you say?' he asked, completely off-balance.

'I said that the sale of the company is at a critical stage,' repeated Gilbert.

'This is all very sudden,' spluttered Eric.

'I know. But circumstances have changed rather dramatically,' he replied.

'Why all the cloak and dagger?' asked Eric, feeling emboldened by the alcohol.

'Look, come and take a seat,' said Gilbert before continuing. 'I have spoken to the Chief Constable about Anna's misadventure. Apparently, her car was stolen and she asked a friend to drive her home. The Chief Constable tells me that you made a statement, denying all knowledge of the accident with the bicycle. You also stated that you recovered her from her wrecked car at approximately 5.15 pm and then took her to your home.' Eric, though slightly intoxicated, knew that the conversation was reaching a conclusion.

'What are you trying to say?' he asked rather forcibly.

'I need to know, old boy, who is telling porkies, and who is telling the truth,' said Gilbert.

Eric laughed, he couldn't stop himself. 'And which version of this charade do you want to believe?' he asked.

'I only want the truth,' said Gilbert, almost in a whisper.

'Well,' said Eric, eyes blazing, 'I can tell you that if this comes to court, my witness statement is the whole truth, and nothing but the truth.'

Gilbert looked devastated. He could tell by Eric's demeanour that he was being truthful. 'This is a bad time for me,' said Gilbert, 'we have a meeting in the morning with the Union shop stewards, and the future is very uncertain for everybody.'

'But not for you,' said Eric to himself, 'you're not

interested in my plans for the future.' The whisky no longer tasted good. He placed his glass on a low table and asked to be driven home.

Eric knew that whichever way the meeting went the next day, Gilbert would come out smiling, ready for the next phase of his progress to the top table, and possibly a knighthood. Back at home, Eric conjectured what the mood would be like when Gilbert spoke to Anna: would she still be adamant that she had had nothing to do with the cyclist's accident?

*

After a restless night, he made his way to work and sat in his office weighing the options that could be available to him, not relishing the thought of facing the furore of the workforce. The dreaded hour came around and he headed towards the Boardroom. Union reps and fellow employees were seated in the front rows of the room. As Eric entered, Gilbert signalled him to sit at the top table.

Once the doors to the Boardroom were closed, Gilbert stood up and welcomed everyone to a 'full and frank discussion'. He spoke of what the company stood for in the eyes of the local populace.

'The world does not owe us a living, and market forces have been squeezing margins tighter and tighter, which means everyone works harder, and longer, for our daily bread.'

A sullen mood descended like a cloud, people started to grumble and fidget. At this point, Gilbert raised the temperature by going for the jugular. He sprayed his audience with facts and figures.

He reiterated that orders were drying up, absenteeism was at its highest level, and the company was only producing 50% of its output of five years before. The new technology that had been installed had had only a minimal effect on production. Finally, the bombshell:

'The unions knew about this situation but have done

nothing to address the decline in output. Based on recent figures supplied by our auditors and confirmed by the bank, the company will be bankrupt in nine months.'

Concluding his statement, Gilbert said, 'Most of the blame lies with the negative attitude of the unions together with an apathetic workforce who did not have the best interests of the company at heart.'

Expecting an uproar, Eric steeled himself, but the response seemed almost muted. There were looks of shock and open mouths. Then voices began to rise, followed by a slow handclapping.

Chapter 12

A shop foreman stood up and asked, 'Is it true that a big order has been tendered for, and acceptance is only a formality?'

Gilbert Stallen responded by saying that he had no such information at the moment, but if the facts were available at a later date, he would inform the staff and workforce in general at once. His answer was met by catcalls and the slow handclap.

Gilbert left the meeting and motioned Eric to follow him. Back in the CEO's office, Eric declined the large whisky offered to him, saying that it was a bit early in the day. Gilbert was elated, however, and didn't hide his enthusiasm, pounding his desk in triumph as he emptied his glass. Eric had his private thoughts as to how well the meeting had gone, but he knew that Gilbert held all the cards. If the unions extended the strike, Gilbert would close the company. On the other hand, in the event of any agreement to return to work, in nine months, the company would be closed due to labour intransigence, and unsatisfactory working practices.

Sensing Eric's reluctance to express any opinion about the meeting, Gilbert asked bluntly, 'How did you think the meeting went, rather better than expected?' Eric countered by asking what his position was in all this controversy. 'Good question,' replied Gilbert. 'Unfortunately, the answer is dependent on how we resolve the dilemma of who was responsible for the unfortunate incident that occurred last week. As you are aware, my relationship with your boss is at a critical point. If your boss, my muse, was convicted of a criminal offence based on circumstantial evidence, we both lose. You would be sacked, or made redundant, and I would lose my soulmate.'

Eric weighed up the consequences to his own self-respect, and the memory of his dear wife, and decided that perjury was not an option. Eric knew that Gilbert enjoyed threatening people, and decided not to show any sign of weakness.

'I stand by my statement of the facts, as I see them, and the whole truth will come out if this incident goes to court.'

Gilbert's eyes narrowed and his face became puce. 'Get out of my office!' he bellowed. Eric smiled, and knew that whatever happened to the company, he would not be beaten by a bully.

*

Back in his own office, he reprised the scenario with Gilbert. He felt elated that he had knocked the man off his pedestal. Suddenly, a knock on his office door brought him back to the present. 'It's open,' said Eric, slightly apprehensive.

A young woman entered the office.

'I'm sorry to disturb you,' she began, 'I'm collecting for Mrs Duckworth's leaving present.' Eric was stunned, a complete beauty had entered his office, and he was immediately smitten. Regaining his composure, he asked when was the lady's last day. 'At the end of this week,' was the reply. 'I'll be glad to,' said Eric.

He took a five-pound note from his wallet and passed it over, the girl's smile was enchanting.

'We're having a party night at the Printer's Arms,' she told him, 'in the function room. All the office staff are going to give her a good send-off. Would you like to come?' Feeling a little embarrassed, Eric nodded and smiled, 'I'd be delighted.'

The rest of the week passed quickly, and the weekend was upon him. After some deliberation, he decided that a night out could enliven his social life and help him to relax and chill out - hopefully in the company of the beautiful girl at the office.

After changing into something smart but casual, he phoned for a black cab. The Printer's Arms was bright and welcoming, and discreet lighting illuminated the hanging baskets at the front of the building.

Chapter 13

On entering the bar, Eric was struck by the buzz that Fridays had always given him. He felt the latent energy stirring, a desire to enjoy the weekend, and no work till Monday.

At the bar, he was ordering a bottle of Pilsner, when a tap on the shoulder made him turn around. It was the young girl from the office. She smiled, and Eric felt a rush of intense pleasure; she looked absolutely gorgeous, her tanned legs and slim waist were set off by a generous cleavage. Her voice was friendly.

'Hello, I'm Sam by the way,' she said. Eric struggled to find words that didn't sound gibberish. Before he could show he'd lost his cool, she gave a little twirl.

'I scrub up well, don't I?' she said without any artifice. Eric felt a rush of adrenaline. 'Absolutely beautiful,' he heard himself say. 'Let me get you a drink,' eager to keep her company.

'Vodka Martini,' said Sam, with a twinkle in her eye.

'Coming up!'

The closeness of her body made him tingle. The delicate fragrance of her and her easy manner had him hooked. After being served by a very pleasant barmaid, he motioned to the staircase that led to the first floor. The music was throbbing, and Eric felt the sensual pleasure of Sam's company.

'Can I introduce you to Yolande, the lady who's leaving us?' said Sam.

They approached a group of laughing guests. Eric was immediately aware of a beautifully coiffured, middle-aged woman, wearing a stunning necklace which radiated reflections of the disco lights. Leaning forward to kiss her on the cheek, he met with her lips instead. A hand gently squeezed his crotch. The sensation was electric, and he gasped with surprise. 'Catch you later,' she whispered invitingly.

Taken aback, he turned towards Sam and led her onto

the dance floor. 'Let's dance,' he said, taking her gently by the arm. He'd sooner spend an hour with Sam than fight off an over-sexed older woman.

The energy level in the room, along with the volume of the music, had risen a thousand per cent, and Eric felt part of it. His heart was pumping hard, and he felt like he had as a teenager. After ten minutes dancing with Sam, the music changed and he found the beat no longer matched his mood.

They went back to their drinks and found a booth in a quieter corner. Sam seemed genuinely interested in his conversation but Eric felt a bit out of his depth, knowing that his taste in music and fashion was dated by modern standards. Trying to stick to non-controversial topics was not easy; Sam liked to talk and was interested in a wide range of subjects.

'I was born in South Africa,' she told him, 'but I was educated in England. My parents were divorced and my mother became withdrawn; she lost her friends and alienated our relatives. It broke her heart I think, and she died within two years.' Eric felt some discomfort at her revelations, and subtly changed the subject.

They had not been talking for more than a minute or two when suddenly the bubble burst as a group of young girls appeared and whisked Sam back onto the dance floor. Eric felt rather foolish, sitting there alone, surrounded by couples enjoying themselves. Moving over to the bar, he ordered a double whisky and water. As he stood sipping his drink and hoping that Sam would reappear, he heard some laughter, and wondered if he was the subject of it. He felt awkward and out of place, and decided to get a taxi home.

*

On the welcome mat inside his front door was a large, white, sealed envelope. Eric felt let down, and a little miffed, that Sam had decided that his company was not as interesting as dancing with her workmates. Putting the envelope on a worktop, he removed his jacket and switched on the kettle. As the kettle heated up, he disinterestedly slit open the envelope. A page of an old exercise book with pasted newspaper cuttings fell out onto the floor. Eric bent down and picked it up slowly, wondering what it could be. The letters, which were cut from various articles with widely varying fonts took a bit of deciphering. Together, they spelt out a message: 'This is part of a bigger picture, get wise or else.'

He suddenly felt very vulnerable. Wondering why he was being targeted, he glanced at Gloria's portrait on the wall; her face seemed to emanate calm and reassurance. The kettle clicked off and as he made himself a cup of tea, he gained some control of his emotions. He took the tea up to bed with him where he longed for the comforting warmth of his wife, but all he felt was cold, empty space.

Although his mind was full of questions, he slept well. At seven-thirty, the light on the bedside phone signalled he had received a voicemail.

'Eric,' said Anna's voice quietly over the speaker, 'we need to talk.' Eric groaned inwardly. He picked up the phone receiver and her voice seemed brittle and weary. 'Gilbert's on leave,' said Anna, 'and the unions are playing a wildcard. Apparently, part of the business was in hock to the employees' Sharesave scheme, and obviously most of the workforce are against any sell-off.'

She told him that an unnamed source had revealed to the Union that the company owned a large tract of land adjacent to the town, which could be used to expand the firm's operations in the future. She continued, saying, 'This knowledge is dynamite in the present situation. Gilbert has told me to get in touch with the Board and senior management.' She paused and then with her voice lowered, she said, 'I need you to give me moral support in my efforts to control this situation. Meet me at the Lawns Hotel in an hour.' Eric wasn't pleased at this news, but as part of senior management, felt that he had no option but to support her.

*

Pulling up on the forecourt of the hotel, his stomach rumbling, he saw Anna arrive in a black limousine.

She was dressed in a black leather jacket with slim, chalk-striped ankle-length trousers, and white bootees. Her face looked drawn and flaky. Eric was shocked to see her so fragile. She walked slowly up the steps to the wide glass doors.

Chapter 14

Eric was directed to a side annexe. On entering the room, he saw a group of bleary-eyed people standing huddled round a portable electric fire. He made his way over to a table near the window with cups and saucers and poured himself a tea. Out of the corner of his eye, Eric saw Anna break away from the group and make directly towards him. 'Nice to see you Eric, thanks for backing me up,' she said with little enthusiasm.

Eric gave her a grudging nod, feeling very peevish and not in a mood for sarcasm. 'I'll introduce you,' she said, almost gushing with civility. As he approached the group with cup in hand, he felt all eyes were on him.

'I've arranged for a quiet room,' she announced to the group, expressionless, 'and I'm assured that the heating will be working.'

Anna opened the meeting. 'As from today, the buck stops at my desk. Our new Personnel Director will be Mr Eric Wilkinson.' Eric was stunned; what was she playing at, springing the promotion on him without any consultation? Trying to keep his cool, after a moment's hesitation he replied directly to her that there would be further discussions before accepting the position.

The agenda carried on with a lot of ego-massaging: people were given new titles, aligned with relocation, met with some objections from a few. After some minor quibbles about relocation, Anna said, 'I've arranged for breakfast to be served in the main dining room.'

As people drifted towards the dining room, Eric hung back, anxious to define what his surprise promotion was all about. He saw Anna and walked over to where she sat at a small bar

'Eric darling,' she cooed in a tone that spelt trouble, 'I need to brief you about what we propose to do about shrinkage.' The penny dropped.

'So that was what all the shuffling and promoting was

about,' said Eric. 'De-stabilising the workforce and then redundancy.' Her face was a rictus smile of fake surprise. 'Not at all,' she replied. 'Only we need to make the company more productive, ready for the Asian rim, and open up our South American contacts.'

'Excuse me,' interrupted Eric, 'this is the weekend, and I do have a life outside of my job.' Her look became icy and Eric was left in no doubt that the future of personal relations was going to be very bleak. He decided to skip breakfast.

Back in his car, he chewed over the scenario that was unfolding. Gilbert had briefed Anna and then moved out of range of the firing line. Eric could see that if he took the promotion, he was the one who would take all the flack. He started the car. Classic FM emanated from the speakers, giving him soothing music, the balm he craved.

As he drove along, he realised he needed something to eat. Driving into a pub car park, he entered and ordered soup and a sandwich. A customer passed Eric a Sunday newspaper as he took a seat at a small table. Glancing at the business section, he noticed a comment about the company share price rising 5p in Friday's trading.

Driving home, he tried to put out of his mind all thoughts of work, and decided that when he got home, he would check out the video he'd had the sense to set up a few days before.

Chapter 15

Watching the video of Anna's movements on his phone, he was surprised at the feeling of elation that it generated. Eric guessed that in a crowded courtroom, Anna would use all her ingenuity and mastery of her emotions to sway the jury round to her version of what took place. The sexual details would be given in a voice of aggrieved submission. Eric hoped the video evidence would support his case.

Suddenly his landline rang. He got up and crossed the room to pick it up. He didn't recognise the voice, but the caller was obviously clued up about him.

'Mr Wilkinson, could I have a word? I'm from the Chronicle.' Eric was shocked.

'Who am I speaking to?' he asked.

'Philip Barton,' was the reply, 'chief reporter. I would just like to get your reaction to some questions that have been asked in Parliament last Friday, regarding rumours of the closure of Stallen Engineering.'

'I think you should address your questions to the CEO', replied Gilbert.

'Unfortunately, he seems to be out of the country,' the reporter replied. Eric decided to stall.

'Give me your number, and I'll get back to you.'

Just then his mobile vibrated on the coffee table. 'Now what?' he almost screamed as he saw Anna's name on the display.

'I'm in a fix,' said his nemesis, her voice harsh and trembling.

'Gilbert's out of the country and can't be reached, the press is breathing down my neck, and all hell has broken out with the unions. I've also had a visit from the police. Apparently, they have a witness statement that a woman was seen driving a black coupé around the time I was going home from the office, shortly before the accident occurred.'

Eric told her to get in touch with her solicitor and make a statement, then he excused himself by saying, 'I need to answer the door.'

*

The following Monday morning, he was met by Anna in the car park outside the office. She appeared to be highly nervous, her eyes were puffy, and her voice very fractured and hesitant.

'Come to my office,' she said almost in a whisper, 'I need to talk.'

Eric shadowed her along the corridor to her inner sanctum. She opened a silver box on her desk and retrieved a king-size cigarette. Eric noticed that her hands were shaking, and he couldn't help feeling a warm glow as he realised that her house of cards was on the point of collapse. Flicking a lighter, Eric lit her cigarette and saw the fierce burning as she inhaled.

Anna sat down in her large comfortable desk chair, leaving Eric standing. Her silence seemed eternal, and the look of concentration on her face formidable. Suddenly she broke out of her reverie.

'I am going away for a while.'

Eric was taken by surprise, and asked, 'Where to?'

'Geneva,' replied Anna.

'You will inform the police?' he said, in his most innocent tone.

'I expect so,' was the reply. She then said, 'Any further discussions about your promotion will be with Gilbert on his return.'

Eric wondered if his meeting with Gilbert just a few days before had been an illusion; was Anna not privy to Gilbert's intentions about the company? Maybe he had better keep his conversation with the CEO close to his chest.

On his way home, he bought a local paper. In it, the Coroner's report on the cyclist's death stated that his blood had contained alcohol. An open verdict was recorded. Eric felt that mitigating circumstances were sliding into the scenario.

Later, while listening to the radio in an armchair, he fell asleep. When he awoke, he went into the garden and dead-headed some roses, a particular favourite pastime of Gloria's.

The evening was darkening, and an early night would help to recharge his batteries. He dreamed of when he and Gloria were on holiday, dancing and laughing together.

The following day he felt a flood of isolation. Had Gloria been there, she would have given him a crushing kiss and made him feel better, her positivity flooding the room.

After a fractious morning at work, he went out for lunch, and decided that he needed to unwind. Later in the afternoon, after checking his diary, he saw that his golf club subscription needed renewing. He decided that a game of golf would boost his morale.

Chapter 16

As he arrived at the golf club car park, he noticed an early model Mercedes with gull-wing doors. It was immaculate and gleaming. As he entered the clubhouse, he saw the bar was open, so he decided to choose one of the guest beers.

A couple was sat facing the green. The woman's voice was familiar, and after a second or so, he realised that it was Sam's. The realisation bowled him over – what an unlikely coincidence! He decided to introduce himself.

'Hello,' he said in his most friendly tone, 'fancy meeting you again.'

Sam spun round, a surprised look on her face.

'Hi,' she answered. Her legs uncrossed and a hint of annoyance flickered on her face.

'Thinking of joining the club?'

Sam replied, 'My friend has invited me to look the place over and see if I would like to join.' She looked stunning in a summery dress with strappy shoes and a chiffon scarf.

Eric felt embarrassed about walking out of the party and wondered if Sam was annoyed about him leaving early. Her body language was rather ambiguous but not unfriendly. The friend was the son of the club Captain.

Eric nodded to the friend. 'We don't see you at the club very often Tony,' he said with veiled contempt.

Tony shifted uncomfortably. 'I spend a lot of my time in London.'

Eric was not convinced, but seeing Sam made him feel energised, and sent the adrenaline pumping through his veins. 'I hope you got home alright on Friday,' said Eric, suppressing a slight irritation in his voice.

Sam smiled, 'Yes thank you, my friends ordered a taxi for me.' After some polite conversation, Eric decided that any meaningful dialogue would be awkward.

'I'll leave you two alone,' he said, and returned to the bar. Later, he saw them leave and waved in their direction.

After joining some members on the green, he had an

enjoyable round of golf. He was invited to stay for dinner, but he needed some time to think what his options were following his conversations with Gilbert and Anna. He also was concerned about how a possible court case might affect his future job prospects.

*

Arriving back at work the following day, he felt a buzz of anticipation, and as he entered the car park, he glanced up and saw Sam looking through one of the windows and felt a tingle of excitement shoot through his body.

At his desk, Eric switched on his PC and saw an e-mail from Colin Dempsey, the company secretary, asking him to drive to Hickling Manor. Hickling was an updated manor house. Wondering what was in store for him, he made enquiries and was told that the CEO had personally requested his presence. A little disappointed that he wouldn't get to speak to Sam that day, he put on his jacket again and set off in his car.

As he entered the Reception area of the manor, he was met by Colin Dempsey who greeted him warmly.

'So glad you were able to come,' he said, gripping his hand firmly. They entered what was grandly called an orangery, marble columns and tastefully decorated plaster-work. Eric felt he must have done something right, or was this just a front to get him on board with the CEO? He was handed a flute of champagne, the bubbles tickling his face. It was excellent, nothing like the supermarket plonk that people used to offer him at wedding receptions. Across the room, Gilbert beckoned him to join the other members of his group. After some polite chit-chat, Gilbert said that, along with other guests, Eric had been invited to the meeting so that he and other key staff would be the first to know what the firm's plans were for the future.

It had been decided that the factory would be closed, rather than waiting for the inevitable, and the site would be used for re-development. Anna was suddenly at his elbow.

‘A good result,’ she said, straight-faced. Eric was furious.

With no attempt to lower his voice, he moved to face her directly and said, ‘You stand there and say that the company is going to close the factory and rip the heart out of the community so that some asset-stripper can slice up the site and turn the town into a shoppers’ paradise?’

Eric couldn’t get out of the car park fast enough, but back home his frustration wouldn’t dissipate, and he churned over the brief conversation with Anna. His only consolation was the thought that maybe, just maybe, his infatuation with Sam might not be total fantasy.

He dialled the phone number that she had given him at the Printer’s Arms. Eric was relieved that she answered quickly.

‘Hello,’ said Eric, feeling slightly foolish, ‘I just wondered if you might be available on Saturday evening, as it’s the Captain’s Gala Dinner at the golf club, and would you like to be my guest?’

‘I’m not sure,’ was the reply. ‘Can I ring you back, we’re rather busy at the moment.’

Feeling slightly dejected, Eric said, ‘Sure, catch you later.’

Chapter 17

Later in the day, he got an e-mail apology from Sam saying, 'I will be very happy to go to the golf club with you on Saturday.' Delighted, he replied to the e-mail, asking for directions to her apartment so he could collect her on the evening of the golf club event.

This roller-coaster of emotions was a new experience for Eric, and he told himself to calm down and not to read more into the relationship than friendship at this stage. Anna was keeping a low profile, but Eric knew she would not give up and would be plotting to inveigle an alibi from him before any court proceedings took place.

Checking his wardrobe, Eric could see that his old tuxedo was very dated. Not wanting to go into town, he contacted an Asian tailor on the internet. He was assured that a new tuxedo would be ready for him in forty-eight hours. The suit was delivered on the appointed day, the fitting was immaculate, and he felt extremely smart and comfortable.

On the Saturday evening, he took a taxi to Sam's apartment. After Eric rang her from his mobile, Sam came out and joined him in the waiting taxi. Her hair was swept up and highlighted. She wore a white coat and her lilac dress was cut just above the knee.

Her smile was enchanting, and she slid close to Eric, which made him tingle. She gently kissed him on the cheek, commenting very favourably on his new tuxedo. Eric took in her wonderful perfume, and said she looked stunning. 'You look very suave too,' she replied, and then, 'I am looking forward to this evening.'

'This is a very desirable area, Sam,' said Eric, tactfully.

'Yes, my father bought the apartment some years ago on advice from a friend who was in finance. It was a good investment.'

After they arrived at the golf club, they were directed to the Roger Pilkington suite, named after the first Captain and benefactor of the club. He had also been an amateur sailor who competed at Cowes. The room had a nautical theme and was lavishly decorated with fine cotton tablecloths and shiny silver candelabras. Round tables were arranged with eight people per table, and the seats were covered in rich blue velvet. People were laughing and obviously impressed with the décor, and their evening attire matched the opulence of the room. Music was provided by a small group of musicians, also attired in evening wear. They played a selection of sea shanties, which added to the nautical theme.

Once seated with a vodka Martini each, she spoke about her father's involvement with Gilbert Stallen. She told Eric that her father had worked as a scientist in a small family-run company in South Africa but became a majority shareholder when his father had died.

He'd had a small team, and through hard work and tenacity, they developed a tool that was sharper and more resilient than a diamond. He floated his idea in South Africa, but no one wanted a substitute for the diamonds that were coming out of the ground, so her father came to England. He was introduced to Gilbert, who said he might be interested in helping him to market his product. He said he could develop a machine to use the cutting tool which, hopefully, would attract interest from the aviation and mining industries.

'Unfortunately, my father died quite suddenly,' said Sam, 'and Gilbert cut off all contact. Our family learned that Gilbert was about to apply for a patent for the technology and rights in his own name. What Gilbert didn't know was that my father had sold 49% of his title for the super cutting technology, and a lot of money had been invested by various groups of entrepreneurs.'

Eric was intrigued as to what her motives were in applying to join Stallen Engineering as an admin temp. Sam replied that she wanted to gain as much information as she could, so that when Gilbert made his move, she could inform the business group in South Africa.

'I understand your motives,' said Eric, 'but I'm at a loss

as to why you're telling me all this.'

Sam, flushed with the excitement of her revelations, said, 'This company needs people who command respect and have integrity, and can give time and energy to turn the company around.'

Just as they were about to enter the dining area, Eric spotted the golf club Captain and introduced Sam. The Captain was most effusive in complimenting her appearance, and Eric basked in the aura of her presence. Sam was very gracious and played down her stunning dress and her allure.

After their meal, they danced and laughed, and Eric was ecstatic; he felt that he would remember the evening for a very long time and was sure that he had met someone who could make him very happy.

The evening passed quickly, and Eric felt he was in heaven. Sam was enchanting and made him feel part of her world. Her sense of fun, and her physical closeness was invigorating. They talked like they had been together for years. This only increased Eric's desire to tell her about himself and be seen to be confident without seeming arrogant or conceited.

Much later, they taxied back to her apartment. After a sweet kiss on the cheek, she said 'Good night.' Eric felt that he had made a good impression and thanked her for her company. The evening had gone marvellously well and Eric was sure that Sam was very happy to see him again. They arranged to meet the following week and discuss her plans for the company.

Chapter 18

Sam had said that considerable backing would be available, if the right kind of talent was found to make the company more viable, and for the workforce to engage with new management. All that was needed was for the company to become more dynamic.

The weekend felt like a holiday. Eric made a point of introducing Sam to members of the golf club and inviting her to play golf with him at the weekend. Now that he and Sam were dating, he felt years younger, and going to work was less of a chore. He looked forward to seeing Sam and discussing what she wanted the company to be in the future.

Back at his desk on the following Monday morning, the phone rang and he knew that Anna was back on form.

'What have you been saying to Gilbert?' she hissed. Eric, not in the mood for this line of questioning replied, 'I don't follow you.'

'Cut the crap,' she spat like an angry cheetah, 'you've told him about us.'

'Not at all,' said Eric trying to gather his thoughts. 'All I said was that I had found you in your car dazed and disorientated. I assumed that would corroborate what you had said to him.'

'You didn't tell him about going back to your house then?'

'Certainly not,' replied Eric, stressing his words to reinforce his comment, and to convey his annoyance at her tone of voice. 'What happened afterwards was a moment's aberration,' said Eric feeling embarrassed.

'A moment's aberration?' she sneered. 'You seemed to release a lot of pent-up energy,' she retorted.

'When I lifted you out of your car, you were in a state of shock, and you needed help.'

'Is that what you call it?' she exploded like a grenade.

Eric knew that her ego had gone into meltdown and decided that he had better quit. He quickly put down the phone and left the office. As his car left the compound, he could see Anna punching the plate glass window of her office suite in a fit of rage.

Later, back in his kitchen, he phoned his solicitor's office and was given an appointment for that afternoon.

*

Seated in the Chambers of his solicitor Brian, the world seemed aeons away: the highly-polished desk, with the inkwells in silver cartouches, and Brian was in an ebullient mood.

'What can I do for you?' he said jovially. Eric relayed the gist of Anna's phone call and added that Gilbert would quite likely employ a team of high-priced lawyers to rubbish his testimony.

'Relax,' said Brian, 'all the evidence backs up what you told the police. Off the record,' said Brian quietly, 'my spy in Chambers tells me that Anna is now saying that she was with a colleague from work that day and didn't want any bad publicity damaging his career.' Eric took a sharp intake of breath. 'Did she say who this person was?'

'No,' said Brian. 'but she may be trying to implicate you in some way.' He went on to say, 'Because she is your immediate boss and you felt some form of loyalty, albeit misplaced, does not detract from your initial act of kindness. Any jury will immediately concentrate on your dilemma, and understand that in the circumstances, the accident could have been horrific. If you had ignored the vehicle, and left your colleague to suffer, possibly die of internal injuries, the effect on your conscience could have been detrimental to your health.'

'This is a hell of a can of worms,' Eric said to Brian, 'how will I defend myself against this bitch?'

'Relax,' said Brian again, 'you will be alright as long as you tell the truth.' Eric was shaken by the new revelation and told Brian what had happened between him and Anna in his house.

Brian was silent for a moment, then said, ‘Do you think that she would admit to seducing you?’

Eric didn’t know what to say, or how a jury would react to this information.

Feeling out of his depth and wrong-footed by Anna, Eric’s imagination started to go into overdrive: a court case with all the trauma, the door-stepping by the press…

Eric heard himself say, ‘I don’t need this Brian.’

‘You have nothing to worry about,’ Brian reassured him.

‘It’s alright for you to say that,’ Eric blurted out, ‘but I’m the one in the witness box, not you.’ Brian tried to pour oil on troubled waters by inviting him to the golf club for a round, but he declined.

Later that afternoon he got a text from Sam, saying she would like to talk.

Chapter 19

He suggested a local hostelry not five minutes from his home where they could talk over dinner. Sam arrived in a taxi not long after him, and Eric went to the entrance door to greet her. He got a soft drink for Sam, and a glass of wine for himself.

'You look tired,' Sam said, almost apologetically.

'Do I?' said Eric, surprised by her intuition. He could tell by her look that she knew he had some worries. He felt compelled to unburden himself. 'Let's order some food and I'll tell you what I can.' They chose a table and both ordered from the à la carte menu.

'I've been to see my solicitor,' he said, immediately regretting his outburst. Sam seemed composed but concerned.

'Is it something you can tell me?' she asked delicately.

Eric paused a few moments before telling her, 'I was involved in an incident that happened a couple of days ago with a colleague.'

'Anna?' she said.

'Yes!' said Eric, 'How did you guess?'

'I was talking to one of the girls in the office before I left for lunch. She said that her boyfriend is a journalist on The Post & Gazette, and he told her that a big story was breaking, involving a female director of Stallen Industries. Well, we both know that Anna is the only female director and her car has not been seen for several days. So… it didn't take much working out.'

Eric let out a groan. 'Oh no,' he said, covering his mouth.

Sam appeared to do a double-take. 'This story – it has nothing to do with you, has it?' she said, almost in a whisper.

'Yes, I'm afraid it has,' said Eric, covered with embarrassment, feeling that all his dreams were about to explode in his face. Sam went quiet for a moment.

‘Have you anything you would like to tell me?’ she said. Not feeling that her involvement would be helpful, or in her own interests, Eric was reluctant to go into any great detail.

‘Suffice to tell you, I am an innocent party in all that has happened.’

He really didn’t want to have Sam delving too closely into what could be a rather messy can of worms.

‘Forget about me,’ he said urgently. ‘What about your day?’

Sam said, ‘Apparently Gilbert has done a runner, and liquidated all his shares. He has also put his mansion up for sale. According to my source,’ she continued, ‘Gilbert has a bolthole abroad, possibly in South America. His father used to export a lot of sophisticated machinery to Paraguay, and besides, the family have many friends and contacts in Argentina.’

To Eric, this information was the result of a lively imagination working overtime. He uttered a silent prayer that her revelations were true however, as it would save him a lot of embarrassment if Anna and Gilbert disappeared for a decade or two.

‘Did you not realise that Gilbert and Anna were lovers?’ said Sam incredulously. Not wanting to be seen to be ingenuous, Eric replied, ‘I did suspect that they had a very tactile relationship.’

Sam laughed. ‘Well, that’s one way to describe it.’

Sam seemed to be excited, and it was obvious she was hoping she could exploit any vacuum created by Gilbert’s absence. But Eric made it clear to Sam that he wouldn’t be railroaded into any decision that could weaken his own financial future. He also advised her that whoever took on Gilbert’s role would have a heavy responsibility, and would need to build bridges between management, staff and the unions. Sam gave him a look of utter sweetness.

‘You are my knight in shining armour,’ she said.

‘Pardon? Whatever do you mean?’

‘Without your help, none of what I propose would have any validity. You have the respect and integrity that people admire, people will listen to you, and feel that whatever you say has the stamp of success.'

Still not convinced that management and staff would go along with her plans, Eric listened to what Sam had to say. He was conscious that he himself had a considerable holding in the company Sharesave option, and wondered if he should cash in before the press had wind of Gilbert's sudden departure.

Chapter 20

Eric had misgivings about Sam's real intentions regarding the company, and her involvement with wealthy South African business people. When she went to powder her nose, he ordered a bottle of the most expensive champagne on the menu. Shortly afterwards, Sam returned with a smile.

'This is a surprise, what are you celebrating?' she said coyly.

'Wait and see,' replied Eric mysteriously.

On her second top-up, she reminded Eric that she had a job to go to.

'As your line manager, I have the final word on whether you need to go back to work,' he said, with a hint of pomposity, 'but I do think a strong black coffee would help to clear our heads.'

As they walked the short distance back to his home, their laughter got louder, and both felt slightly euphoric. Behind the closed front door, her hand touched his face, and her lips were cool and inviting. She pressed her hips closely to Eric; the erotic smell of her perfume added a dimension that reprised his role with Anna. Sam slipped off her shoes, her slim legs and ankles adding to a sensual excitement coursing through his veins and propelling an erection of intense pleasure inside his pants. Eric scooped Sam into his arms and carried her upstairs with alacrity, into the master bedroom. His hand found the zip at the top of her dress and it glided down her smooth, arched back.

Her hands had opened his flies and slipped inside his trousers, her touch on his member was cool and gentle. She kissed him tenderly, his whole body was in thrall to her touch. Releasing her from her bra, Eric was amazed at her lovely firm breasts which tilted slightly upward, with rather large nipples. She giggled as he kissed the hard-pink protuberance. Pushing her knickers off her peach-like buttocks, Eric knew that this moment would stay in his imagination for the rest of his life. Gently removing her remaining clothes, he pressed her softly down onto the bed, and positioned himself between her gorgeous thighs. His penetration was smooth and mind-blowing, her legs embraced his body tightly, their union was total and she didn't hold back. He was consumed by Sam's desire to extract all manner of sexual excitement and release from her lover. Her tongue was in his mouth and Eric was ecstatic, his body trembling with excitement and lust. Suddenly Sam's movements became quite frenzied and Eric guessed that her orgasm was imminent. Sam gasped and cried out, her body heaving and gripping him intensely. Eric moaned, as he felt his own exquisite thrill and release inside her vagina.

After a few moments, they unwound their bodies from each other and lay on the bed, happy and content. Eric couldn't believe what had just happened. He deliberately pinched himself and laughed out loud.

As he began to doze, he felt her weight lift off the bed.

'Are you OK?' he asked.

'Yes,' she replied, 'I need to use the bathroom.'

Eric suddenly felt alone; he rose from the bed, anxious for her company. As he entered the bathroom, she turned and kissed Eric, the smooth touch of her yielding flesh sent shivers of excitement through the whole of his body.

'Come and have a shower,' she said, almost breathlessly. Again Eric was overcome with an intoxicating desire for sexual satisfaction. Sam's energy was astonishing as she led him into the enveloping warmth of the shower. Eric revelled in her passion and her red-blooded sexual hunger.

Later in the kitchen, she made him an omelette and sat on his knee. Their matching bathrobes gave Eric a moment of *déjà vu.* Sam was feeding him in a slow and tantalising fashion. Eric wanted the moment to last for eternity; even now, the warmth of her body conjured up a feast of wild and abandoned sexual gymnastics, but his logical mind made him ask, 'What's next?'

Sam held his face in her hands and kissed him sweetly.

‘I need you to answer that question,’ she replied. Eric knew that his answer could mean a relationship, or a chasm of uncertainty. Looking into her eyes, he realised that life with her would be a wonderful adventure.

‘I want to commit to us,’ said Eric, ‘you have opened my eyes to an exciting and loving partnership. And together, we could conquer the world.’

He held his breath, not knowing what her reaction might be, but the dazzling smile on her face filled the void in his heart.

Chapter 21

When Sam's mobile beeped, Eric groaned silently. Within ten minutes a car arrived to pick her up. Eric walked her to the end of the drive.

As she swung her slim legs into the car, Eric bent down and kissed her tenderly on the lips. As the car moved off down the road, she blew him a kiss. Watching the car disappear beyond the trees, he hoped that the old emptiness would not return, her presence had filled the void to overflowing.

Later, when the euphoria had passed, Eric was consumed with doubts, and wondered how he was going to face a courtroom of people. They would probably think he had taken advantage of a victim of an horrific accident, who needed help and consideration, not vilification. Whichever way he played it, Eric was convinced Anna would try to crucify him in court.

He resolved to tell Sam about the details of his sexual liaison with Anna in full; he prayed she would understand that the encounter was only momentary. How to arrange a suitable venue to meet with Sam consumed him for the rest of the evening, but he was spared making a decision as she contacted him the following day.

'I need to go back to South Africa for a family conference. I'll be away for ten days or so,' she told him.

Her absence gave Eric time to establish if some agreement would be possible with Anna's defending Counsel. He needed to release the pressure that was building but didn't know how. He decided to talk to Brian, his brief. He knew that he was clutching at straws but was willing to try anything to save his relationship with Sam.

*

'I wonder if we could describe the events after the accident without going into the intimate details of what had happened at the house. What procedure will the police follow?' he asked Brian.

'You will be made aware,' said Brian, 'of any accusations being made against you by the defendant. This will be left on the file till such time as all evidence has been scrutinised by the defendant's barrister or brief. Then the prosecution will need to interview you, with a view to corroborating the statement that you made to the police. It appears that no witnesses have come forward, as regards you removing Anna from her car. It will be your word against hers. She, on the other hand, says that you were driving her home as her car had been stolen. This is the story she has told the police.'

Eric again felt out-manoeuvred by Anna's scheming, even when she was only half-conscious. Her wily brain had created an alibi for every detail of her treachery. Eric was appalled to think what the prosecution would say about her being in his home, particularly her revelations about their sexual coupling, and how it had affected their relationship.

A black hole was opening up before Eric's eyes, and he had no defence against all the evidence that confronted him.

'If only I'd had the sense to push her down the stairs, none of this would be happening,' he thought, miserably.

*

As the days moved forward, he wracked his brains for anything that would extricate him from this mess. Brian, his solicitor, did make him aware of the due process of law, and felt confident that the court would be lenient as regards his entanglement with Anna. But Eric was more concerned with the effect that the revelations would have on his relationship with Sam. How was he going to explain that what had happened was due to his lack of emotional stability, and just an outlet for his natural instincts? The court proceedings would drag on, and his self-esteem would take a battering.

*

There was no mention forthcoming in the court papers of whether Anna had told Gilbert what had happened at Eric's house. He held onto the slender chance that Gilbert was unaware of their sexual liaison. Trying not to focus on what the court would hear, Eric tried to prepare his story for Sam when she returned from South Africa.

As the week passed, Eric felt his nerves stretching to breaking point. Sam had taken Eric on a journey of enlightenment. She had broached the subject of his moving into her apartment on a trial basis for three months, and if the relationship was still growing, then they could look for some permanent base in the UK.

Chapter 22

The ten days seemed to fly by, and then they were together again, and enjoying all the events that their busy lives had developed. Sam had practicality and foresight which appealed to Eric's sense of order. The only sticking point was that he had not yet had the courage to tell Sam about Anna; this neglect began to eat into his conscience. The time never seemed right, and he was desperate for the relationship to be cemented in a positive way.

Life with Sam was magical. He was enthralled by her beauty and her femininity, she completely encapsulated all that he could wish for in a soulmate. She supported him and gave him confidence, but the thought that he could lose her undermined his resolve to come clean about Anna.

As the time of the arraignment gathered pace, Eric became more and more desperate. He knew that he would have to face the scenario that was going to be played out in court. He must tell Sam the full facts before the press released all the lurid details into the public domain. He decided to engineer a weekend when they could be together on neutral ground so that neither of them would feel intimidated if the revelations spilled over into a total breakdown of their relationship.

Eric wanted to surprise Sam and put the best possible conditions forward to soften the impact when he made her aware of what had happened with Anna in a moment of madness. Whichever way he put it, he knew that Sam's feminine intuition would dismiss any false protestations that he used to influence her decision. He decided that a full and frank declaration of the facts was his only option with any chance of feeling a sense of catharsis about his conduct. He had spoken to Sam the previous weekend about spending a few days together in the Lake District. She had agreed that it would be a wonderful opportunity to get out into the fresh air and see a part of the country that she wasn't familiar with.

He booked a suite for three nights at a prestigious hotel overlooking Lake Windermere. He felt that his best chance of resolving his dilemma could be strengthened if Sam felt his intention had been purely to help Anna, with no motive of a sexual nature. As the weekend approached, Eric prayed that his fears of an end to his romance with Sam would prove groundless.

They spoke about the plans for the journey and agreed that they would travel in the morning, stopping for lunch before arriving at their hotel. He knew that the Lakes were a magnet for people wanting a break from the daily grind and they agreed that Friday morning would be an opportune time to make their journey more agreeable.

*

About half past nine on the Friday morning, Eric arrived at the block of imposing apartments. He was hoping that the bulk of the rush-hour traffic would have arrived at their destinations. Before getting out of the car, he phoned Sam's mobile and she answered slightly breathlessly. 'Come up to the flat,' she said, laughing, 'I'm still in the shower!'

Eric was hoping that Sam would be ready to go but realised that women have their own agenda. He entered the door she'd left slightly open for him and called his greeting, but she didn't reply. Eric could hear the shower running.

In the open-plan kitchen, he switched on the kettle. A mug was on the breakfast table and he made himself a coffee. Waiting patiently for Sam to finish getting ready, he moved towards the picture window and sipped his coffee. He felt totally awed by the panoramic view.

'I'm sorry for the delay,' said Sam's voice behind him, 'but I didn't get back from London till 1am.' Eric was stunned at Sam's wonderful figure, she looked so delicious standing there in bra and knickers, he couldn't believe his good fortune. Her smile made him tingle all over his body.

'No problem,' said Eric cheerfully, 'hopefully, the heavy traffic will be well on its way by now.'

‘Could you make me a coffee?’ she purred, approaching him for a kiss. ‘I’ll have it black,’ she said, ‘it might boost my metabolism.’ Eric smiled to himself, he felt ten feet tall. ‘What a wonderful day,’ he said.

A few minutes later Sam came back into the room, wearing black slacks and a ribbed, fluffy white sweater that clung to her breasts. She gave a little twirl and said, ‘Will I pass muster?’ Eric was goggle-eyed.

Chapter 23

Suppressing his mounting desire for her, he suggested they set off for the Lakes.

'Give me five minutes,' replied Sam, and disappeared into the bedroom. Eric began to feel impatient but decided to bite his tongue and sank into one of the sumptuous armchairs.

Sam had a wonderful ability to match her ensemble to the occasion. A minute later, she came out of the bedroom in a Barbour coat, perfect for country walking. Again, Eric was elated by her choice of clothing, she looked stunning. Eric picked up her case, already packed.

Going down in the lift, she gave him a quick kiss and he pulled her close. 'You look so beautiful,' he said. 'Thank you, sir,' she replied with a cheeky grin.

Eric felt that he had turned a corner in his life, but the nagging worry that it could all come crashing down made him more determined than ever to convince Sam that he was the innocent party.

*

Once they had reached the motorway, he asked Sam what type of music she liked to listen to.

'Middle of the road,' she answered, 'perhaps leaning to romantic ballads and country music.' Again, Eric experienced a sense of *déjà vu* - Gloria had had a similar preference. Eric tuned into an easy-listening request show and was delighted when he heard 'Wichita Lineman' over the air waves.

Sam gushed when she heard Glen Campbell's voice. 'I do like to hear a good Country and Western,' said Eric, singing along to the tune. Sam joined in with a very sweet sound, making a tear come into his eye.

*

They made good time and eventually came off the M6, heading towards the A591. After stopping for lunch at Sizergh Castle, it wasn't long before they were checking in to the hotel in Windermere. On checking in at the hotel, the receptionist was very friendly and made them feel special. The room had a panoramic view of the lake and was expensively furnished. Eric was delighted that it also included a very enticing Jacuzzi.

Eric was preparing himself to tell Sam about the looming court case, and hoped that the weekend away from the office would give them some breathing space. He was petrified that someone he knew might turn up at the hotel, but hopefully, his gamble of picking a very expensive location would insulate them from stumbling across any colleagues. He had decided that Sunday afternoon would be a good time to make Sam aware of the facts. This was dependant on their two nights together having strengthened their relationship and things being calm and equable.

Running the conversation through his mind, he tried to make his involvement with Anna seem as tenuous as possible, but he also knew that Sam’s intuition would dissect any artifice that he tried to construct. He finally decided that he had better get used to the possibility of losing Sam after he told her about the incident.

After lunch, they decided to drive out to a campsite where Eric had spent a fortnight with some schoolfriends years before. He spoke to someone in the site office, who told him that quite a lot of schoolchildren visited the site from abroad. Eric asked if they could look around and they were told that some refurbishment was going on and the camp wouldn’t be officially open for some weeks, but they could have a look round if they wished.

As they strolled around the site, he was drawn back to his childhood, and remembered the zipwire that allowed the children to travel across half the site, and the large yacht called the Banshee which they had sailed on Lake Windermere one glorious afternoon. He recalled the friendships he had made, and the banter he had enjoyed whilst in their company.

Again, he felt a lot of reassurance from Sam as she listened and seemed genuinely interested.

*

They dressed smart-casual for dinner and Eric was struck by how easily Sam was able to look ravishing with the simplest accessories. The meal was excellent, and Eric had ordered a bottle of champagne which he thought was very good, and nicely chilled. The hotel restaurant was not too busy, so they got very good service.

After the meal, they listened to a pianist who had a very romantic back-catalogue. Sam sang along to a number of the tunes and Eric was thrilled. The evening was magical, and he wanted it to be as memorable as possible. He wanted to see Sam smile and laugh for eternity. All his future dreams hung on how he presented his version of the events following Anna's car accident. He knew that if his sincerity and honesty didn't seem genuine, he had no hope of any future happiness with Sam. She had won his heart and filled his thoughts in such a manner that he felt her loss would devastate all his emotional desires and leave a chasm that couldn't ever be filled in his lifetime.

Chapter 24

The two of them left the bar area with happy hearts. Sam glowed, and Eric was euphoric.

Upstairs in their suite, Sam disappeared into the bathroom, and Eric lay on the bed expectantly and closed his eyes.

Eric started when he heard Sam laugh loudly.

'Well I didn't expect you to fall asleep so quickly!' she said, half-mocking and with a wry smile on her face. Looking a vision of loveliness, Sam pounced onto the bed and snatched Eric's bed shorts off his legs. 'You won't need these!' she said triumphantly. Eric blushed with total embarrassment. 'Sorry,' he blurted out, 'the wine must have gone to my head.'

'I hope it hasn't affected your capacity to excite me,' she said coyly.

'Not in the least,' he said with more bravado than he felt.

Sam was fully energised and kissed him fiercely, her tongue penetrating his mouth, her cool fingers caressing his stiffening penis. Eric gasped with shock and delight, her boldness making him reassess his own lovemaking technique.

Her thighs squeezed his hips and lifted his body off the bed, making him penetrate Sam deeper than he thought possible. Eric could hear Sam's breathing grow louder, and his own breath was quickening with every thrust. Her pelvic muscles were very strong, and she made Eric feel that he needed to exercise more. He caressed her hard nipples and Sam closed her eyes. He pulled her closer and kissed her fiercely. Moving his hands down to her firm buttocks, he found the crease and gently separated the silky skin to allow his fingers to penetrate her clitoris from behind. This move seemed to energise Sam still further, and she pulled harder on Eric's penis.

Both bodies were now glistening with their combined effort, but Eric knew that he had to surprise Sam with his sexual energy and make her realise that age wasn't a barrier to satisfying a much younger woman.

Sam's orgasm was prolonged and all-embracing. Immediately, his own orgasm followed, vindicating his ability to pleasure Sam and to find his own satisfaction with a woman he loved.

As they both lay back in a state of bliss, Eric felt the exhilaration mingling with guilt. He wanted to be free of any feelings he had for Anna, but he was also still cherishing the memory of Gloria. Eric wanted to share with Sam his innermost thoughts, the pricking of his conscience, his satisfaction of manly pride. Again, he quashed the thought, not wanting to end the exultation that swam inside him. Just a few more hours and then he would tell her the truth.

Switching off the lights, the darkness wrapped them both in a cloak of softness, making Eric feel wanted and fulfilled. Whatever happened in the morning, he would treasure this night of passion for eternity. He dreamed of Gloria, and felt her love and blessing on his commitment to Sam.

*

This feeling stayed with him when he awoke the next morning. The sun was streaming into the room and Sam was in the shower. Eric felt elated, and he was tempted to rush into the bathroom and surprise her. The thought quickly evaporated as he remembered his pledge to himself to come clean about the car accident and its aftermath.

Getting out of bed, he opened the window and felt the warm rays of the sun, and a gentle breeze on his skin. He waited till Sam emerged from the bathroom, and kissed her gently, feeling her moist hair on his face. She gently caressed his semi-erect penis and smiled.

'Still feeling frisky?' she asked coyly. Eric stammered, taken aback by her self-assurance.

'Whenever you are,' he countered.

Sam laughed. ‘You certainly had a lot of passion last night, I wondered if you had taken a little pill or something.’

‘Life in the old dog yet, you mean,’ said Eric.

‘Not at all,’ Sam said, ‘just surprised how energised you were. Shall we have breakfast on the balcony?’

‘Yes please,’ said Eric, ‘that would be lovely.’

Eric phoned for room service and arranged for the food to be brought to their room. The balcony gave them a panoramic view of the hotel grounds and the lake. Sam sat on Eric’s knee in the warm sunshine while they waited.

A knock on the door signalled their breakfast had arrived. Eric ushered in a waiter who brought a trolley laden with a fabulous breakfast, with a bottle of bubbly he had specifically asked for.

Chapter 25

Sam was delighted with the food and the drink, giving Eric a sweet kiss that made him glow with delight. But his mood changed when he saw from the balcony a familiar number plate on a car parked a hundred yards to the right of the hotel car park.

He did a double-take when he realised that the car was a black coupé. What was going on? Surely fate was working overtime. He groaned inwardly, knowing that all his carefully laid plans were about to fall into ruins. Of all the cruel luck, he moaned inwardly.

He must have looked a picture, because Sam asked him if he felt ill. He apologised and said that he was fine, just a twinge in his back. Sam didn't look convinced, but he laughed it off saying he needed more exercise.

Eric made small talk as he attempted to eat his breakfast, but his appetite was gone and he knew the sparkle had gone out of his voice. Sam also seemed more subdued and less upbeat. Feeling a need to explore the hotel, he spoke to Sam and said he was going to get tickets for the boat that went across the lake. 'OK,' she said quietly, 'that would be great.'

Eric was quietly concerned that maybe his change of mood could impact on any later discussions. He moved very quietly around the hotel, being careful not to draw attention to himself. But after ten minutes, he could see no sign of the black coupé. Going back to the room, he took a deep breath and told Sam, 'I didn't get the boat tickets. I need to know your thoughts on a very pressing matter that I need to discuss with you.' Sam was obviously intrigued, and saw that whatever it was, it obviously had had a very subdued effect on his mood.

Eric made sure that Sam was comfortable. He took a chair opposite Sam on the balcony and took both her hands in his. He found it hard to meet her eyes. He began by telling her how remorseful he felt about what had happened, but that with hindsight, there was not a lot he could do about the situation he found himself in. Starting at the beginning, he mentioned his visit to his wife's grave, followed by the events up until Anna had jumped out of his car and legged it back to her home.

Sam was very quiet for some time and was obviously shocked at the revelations. Then she said, 'You must have felt very bad about what did happen.'

Eric was slightly relieved at her concern for his predicament, but also wanted her assurance that she understood that he loved her totally, not Anna. He saw that her body language had changed subtly, and Eric was half-expecting a rebuttal of her feelings towards him.

'I know it must be a shock to hear all this, but I felt I had to be honest and speak to you now, before it all comes out in the press.'

Sam seemed to recover her composure. 'Sorry,' she said, 'I was thinking about how we are going to present this when your court appearance comes up.'

'We?' said Eric, thunderstruck. 'Are you sure you still want to be involved in my messy affairs?'

'We are a team,' she said, with conviction, squeezing his hands hard, 'and don't you forget it!'

Eric felt hot tears in his eyes. What a truly remarkable reaction, totally unexpected.

'I don't know how to thank you,' he whispered.

Sam smiled. 'You have got to be proactive in your defence,' she said. 'All that happened was a culmination of the shock of what could have been a truly horrific accident. You lost control of how you would normally react and were forced by circumstances to be manipulated by a very powerful woman. She used her influence over your position in the company to further her deception and pass on the consequences of what she had done to you in a very underhand and wicked way.'

Eric felt that Sam had a total grasp of his predicament and had got right to the nub of what Anna was trying to do.

'First of all, we need to destroy her alibi,' said Sam, 'then find out who her friends are that she will try to recruit to build her case against you.'

Eric felt the tension melting away. He surely had found a true soulmate in Sam.

'I've contacted my solicitor and made him aware of my suspicions about Anna's motives.'

'We need some hard facts though,' said Sam. 'I know a very good private detective, and I will do some sifting of any relevant facts, that I can glean from my work colleagues.'

Chapter 26

Eric felt the adrenaline buzz that had first attracted him to Sam, and he hugged her with a passion. 'We are a team!' he said, grinning. He had an overwhelming sensation of liberation from his old life. The sun shone on the lake, and he wanted to shout like a football fan whose team had scored the winning goal in the FA cup.

A knock on the door made Eric jump and brought him back to reality.

'A message for Mr Wilkinson,' said the bellboy. Eric took the envelope and thanked him.

Opening the envelope, he found it contained a newspaper cutting of the report of the accident in which the cyclist had died. A phone number written by hand was at the bottom. Sam asked to see the article. 'Someone is keeping a close watch on your movements, so we had better be vigilant.'

Eric felt a shiver of fear run down his back and thought about the envelope he had received previously at home - the letter on his doormat made up of cut-out letters.

'We need to contact that number,' said Sam, 'but let's not panic. First speak to Brian, your solicitor; he may want you to have proof of the phone call, and maybe a recording of the conversation.'

Eric agreed, this seemed an eminently sensible idea, and he called Brian straight away. They agreed to set up a three-way conversation with Brian listening in, but this would necessitate their being in Brian's office. Eric was desperate to continue the weekend with Sam, particularly as the weather promised to be warm and clear, but he knew that contact must be made or a vital link that they were seeking could be lost.

At the hotel Reception, Eric and Sam gathered information regarding travel links within the area. It was suggested that the motorways could be gridlocked due to the fine weather and a sailing regatta that was being staged on the lake that afternoon. Maybe a phone call to a local railway heritage site might give them an opportunity to connect with the national rail network. That way they could enjoy an afternoon together, as well as meeting up with Brian and still be back to the hotel in time for dinner.

Eric called the office of the heritage railway station and discovered that they were running a few special steam trains that weekend for a charity event. The line would link with the national rail network and get them to Brian's within the hour. They set off almost immediately for the heritage railway.

Within half an hour, they were on a Castle class 4-6-0 steam locomotive and bowling along at a good speed for a steam train built early in the 20th century.

Sam seemed totally thrilled, leaning out of the open carriage window, her strawberry-blond hair blowing in the breeze and puffs of steam from the engine.

Eric was totally enrapt at her enthusiasm. He was overjoyed that his worries about her learning the truth about Anna were resolved in such a way that he could feel exonerated and not condemned for his lapse of judgement. The more time he spent with Sam, the more he felt blessed by each wonderful moment in her company.

*

After approximately forty-five minutes, the train pulled into a rather old-fashioned station and they alighted. Over a crackly tannoy system, a voice gave directions for people who wanted to continue their journey onwards. Eric was eager not to lose any time in boarding the next train and the second rail journey had them in the town centre in fifteen minutes.

Eric hailed a taxi at the station forecourt, as the area was busy with shoppers and football fans eager to get to the stadium for a derby match with the local team. He gave instructions to the cabbie and they were off.

'After we've seen Brian, we can stop off here for a late lunch if you like, before we get back on the steam train?'

suggested Eric.

'Why not?' agreed Sam, 'it's pretty here.'

*

Brian's office was out of town, situated in a rather exclusive avenue near to where Eric had gone to school. As the taxi approached the Victorian detached double-fronted building, Eric was impressed by the beautiful garden with borders of bright flowers and sculpted lawns. He began to worry that Brian might object to Sam being privy to what was a very serious situation.

After speaking into the intercom, the door buzzed, and they entered the building. In front of them was a lift. Brian welcomed them as the lift doors opened on the second floor.

'Please come through to my office,' he said, in a very welcoming voice. Eric introduced Sam and explained that she was privy to all the details surrounding the accident and the involvement with Anna. Brian showed them to comfortable sofas facing each other in a well-lit and pleasant room.

'Very well,' said Brian, 'then we can get down to business. First of all, do you know who gave the message to the bellboy?'

'According to the Concierge,' said Eric, 'a tall clean-shaven man dressed in a blazer, with white flannel trousers and a regimental tie, approached the hotel desk and said that he had an urgent message for a Mr Wilkinson from his employers. He handed over the envelope and then left very abruptly.'

'Let me see the cutting,' said Brian. After a few moments perusing the newspaper article and the handwritten note, he commented, 'Not much to go on, but someone clearly knows your every move. Who do you think could be so well-informed of your movements?'

Eric was perplexed.

Chapter 27

'I haven't a clue,' he said. 'It can only have been someone who has trailed me from my home, possibly a private detective, or they may have fitted some device to my car and traced me that way.'

'Someone who maybe wants you to know that they are very concerned about your involvement in the death of that cyclist.'

'Just as well I made a statement when I did,' said Eric.

Carefully entering 141 beforehand so as to block the outgoing number to the recipient, Brian dialled the scribbled number, and indicated to Eric to pick up the extension phone. The phone rang and rang until a recorded message said, 'Thanks for calling. Leave your name and number, and I'll get back to you.'

Eric put down the phone extension. 'This is going to be a hard slog,' he commented. 'I think we are going to have to babysit a public phone booth, one not too obvious, in a quiet area.'

'There is the public booth inside the factory,' suggested Sam, and as I'm on the admin team, I have a key!'

'Brilliant!' replied Eric, 'Why didn't I think of that? It should be quiet on the weekend, only security staff will be on duty, and no one's doing overtime.'

Brian lent them his car. As they drove into the compound of the factory, Eric prayed that the security staff wouldn't clock the number but accept his security pass and Sam's without noting they were not in a company car. As they drove up to the gates, Eric flashed his security card through the open window. The guard gave a cursory glance, then carried on reading his paper as the bar lifted to let them in the compound. 'Just as I thought,' said Eric, as they drove round to the back of the office building.

On entering the main office complex, they found the canteen was locked, but the public phone was situated in an alcove just off the corridor, with a small overhead enclosure. Eric dialled the number that Brian had called not long before, and this time, left a message, not inserting 141.

Eric looked at Sam gratefully as she took his hand and led him to a couple of hard-back chairs along the corridor wall.

The time seemed to drag as they waited for a call back and Sam felt her stomach growling. Suddenly the phone rang: it was another cryptic message.

'Meet me at the Swan with Two Necks in Cowan Bridge at 8pm tonight,' said the voice, 'sit near the bar.' Eric looked puzzled as he felt the voice was familiar. He was convinced that the speaker's voice was opening a door in his memory.

*

'So much for a late lunch!' said Eric. 'Looks like we need to be back on the road as Cowan Bridge is about twenty-five miles from here – would an early dinner at the Swan be OK with you instead?' Sam's smile was all he needed so they left the factory and set off.

*

Arriving at the Swan with Two Necks later that afternoon, they enjoyed an excellent fish and chip meal and then settled down and tried to relax in the bar as agreed with the mysterious caller. In case things turned nasty, Brian had arranged for an ex-police sergeant to be seated unobtrusively in the bar. But Eric could not have been more surprised by the entrance of a man around forty years of age, who ordered a double whisky at the bar. Eric gasped. He was a former colleague who had been his best man at his marriage to Gloria.

The man strolled across and joined Eric and Sam at their table. 'Hello Eric, long time no see,' was the breezy introduction. Eric, still startled, couldn't speak for a couple of seconds, then gulped, 'Tom, I never expected you to turn up! Is this this your local?'

Tom, smiling broadly, shook Eric's hand warmly, then said, 'Are you going to introduce me to the ravishing creature next to you?' Eric introduced Sam who smiled broadly.

'No, it isn't my local,' said Tom, 'I've been following your story in the papers and I just wanted to tell you that you have nothing to fear from Anna's court case.'

Eric was bemused. 'How come you know all about her?'

'It's a long story,' said Tom, 'but I knew Anna many years ago. I don't want her to mess up your life like she did mine. Suffice to say, I am now happily married and I have no bitterness towards her. Unfortunately, she hasn't changed for the better, and so I decided that I would make it my business to get to the truth of your involvement with Anna. I also work as a freelance journalist, and the case will make good copy.'

Eric invited Tom to pull up a stool and join them while he told them all he knew about Anna's antics.

*

When Eric and Sam were back on the road to Brian's, they ran through the options that could be available to them for the court hearing. Eric knew that his evidence and protestations would look very hollow if confronted by Anna's masterly performance as a helpless female in a state of undress. Sam reminded Eric of the private detective she knew. 'He's very discreet, but very expensive,' she added. Eric agreed they should employ him and was adamant that cost was a minor worry when his future hung in the balance.

Sam held his hand and said, 'Don't worry, we'll crack this fiasco, and you'll come up smelling of roses.' Eric nerved himself to be positive.

Chapter 28

As Eric handed the car keys back to Brian, he thanked him for his support and realised that he felt happier than he had expected to. The good reception he had received from Tom made him feel he was closer to a conclusion than he had anticipated. Brian kindly drove them back to the station to get the last train back to their hotel.

When they arrived off the train in Windermere, they were tired after their busy day, and although it was late, Eric insisted that they had a drink in the hotel bar and he ordered two large gin and tonics. Sam drank only half of hers then said she was going up to their room. Eric finished his drink, and a few minutes later, followed her up to the bedroom. There was a moment as he was walking along the corridor when he thought he heard a familiar woman's voice, strident and annoyed. He listened intently but could not quite identify the muffled voice.

Back in the bedroom, Eric saw through the delicate blinds covering the window, a black coupé exiting the car park, and he felt quite euphoric. 'I hope she doesn't come back,' he said to himself.

They had a light supper, and the resident pianist accompanied the diners with a selection of familiar tunes. Sam was looking stunning and the waiters fluttered round her like moths to the flame. She took it in good part, and she obviously enjoyed the attention. Eric was ecstatic and felt very blessed.

*

On Sunday morning, they had a leisurely, late breakfast, then Eric suggested they drive over to Coniston Water and have a sail on the steam yacht 'Gondola' and take in the scenery.

Sam was thrilled, and hugged Eric excitedly. 'That would be marvellous!' she cried. Now that Eric had discovered an ally in Tom and had his mind put at rest, he felt far more relaxed and wanted to make the most of their last day on the Lakes with Sam.

Later in the afternoon, they visited a motor museum, which also housed a replica of the Bluebird speedboat which Sir Donald Campbell had crashed whilst trying to break the water speed world record.

Their last evening was spent in the hotel restaurant enjoying a sumptuous meal with vintage champagne. Eric felt completely in awe of Sam, and that she alone had converted him to a stronger positive mental attitude. He regarded their future life together as a dream certain to come true.

The journey back home on the Monday morning was stress-free, and they were able to drive in a leisurely manner after breakfast.

Chapter 29

As the weeks passed, with factory meetings disrupting productivity on a daily basis, Eric saw many Union officials and disaffected customers come to the factory. Anna seemed to be unconcerned about all the tension among the workforce.

With Sam's careful probing, Eric was able to gather a picture of what Anna was trying to accomplish with the help of her associates. According to an overheard phone call, Anna was dreading Gilbert finding out what had happened between her and Eric. Anna needed to know if he would still want her if she told Gilbert the facts of her indiscretion, but Gilbert was incommunicado. The private detective, on the other hand, had established that on the day in question, Anna was seen coming out of a hotel bar and did seem unsteady on her feet; she dropped her keys, and fell over the front of the car as she tried to retrieve them. One of the bar staff had gone out to her and offered to get her a taxi. Apparently, she was a regular, and she was known among the staff for her frequent drinking and driving.

*

The day of the court summons arrived. Brian had told Eric that Anna would be charged with dangerous driving, with an alcohol level in her blood over the statutory limit whilst in charge of a motor vehicle. Eric had been dreading this moment, and he felt totally dejected. But he called Brian and let him know that he was feeling confident. The truth was Eric felt far from confident, and he called Sam for moral support. Sam told him to focus on the positive and repeat the words that he had already given to the police.

Eric stood in the witness box. The prosecuting Counsel began with Eric's original police statement.

'You said that you came across a black coupé that was

slewed off the road, and that you recognised the registration plate of the vehicle.'

'Yes,' said Eric.

'And is the owner of that registration in court today?'

'Yes,' confirmed Eric, 'the defendant, Ms. Ridley-Pollack.'

'And is the defendant your immediate boss?' said the Counsel.

'Yes, she is.'

'Did you decide to investigate what had happened to the occupant of the car?'

'Yes,' said Eric, beginning to feel uncomfortable at the questioning.

'And whom did you find inside the car?'

'It was Ms. Ridley-Pollack herself.'

'Was she conscious?' asked the Counsel.

'I tried to get an answer but she didn't reply so I assumed she was unconscious.'

'What did you do then?' asked the Counsel.

'I picked her up and took her back to my car.'

'Why didn't you phone for an ambulance'? asked the Counsel.

'There was a heavy storm overhead and torrential rain and there was no signal on my phone.'

'When you eventually got her in your company car, was she still unconscious?'

'No,' said Eric.

'Did you consider getting her to a hospital?'

'Yes, I did,' said Eric, 'but she expressly forbade me not to.'

'Why do think she didn't want you to take her to hospital?'

'I really don't know,' said Eric.

'Was there any alcohol in the car?' probed the Prosecutor.

'I saw no bottles, opened or not,' replied Eric.

'Did you notice a smell of alcohol on her breath?'

Eric replied, 'Yes, it did smell strongly of alcohol.'

‘And when you got to your home, did you phone the police?’

‘No, Anna was vehemently against it,’ said Eric.

‘What did you think might be the consequence of your ignoring her command?’

‘Well, she’s my boss…’ said Eric.

‘So you feared your career would be in jeopardy?’

‘Most certainly,’ said Eric.

‘When you got home, what happened next?’ asked the Counsel.

‘I found some old clothing of my late wife’s and sent her upstairs to get changed while I made us both a coffee and got changed myself.’

‘Did you not demand that you phoned for an ambulance?’ said Counsel.

'Yes, I did,’ said Eric.

‘And what was her reply?’

‘She said that she wanted a cigarette.’

‘Did you offer her a cigarette?’

‘No, I don’t smoke,’ said Eric.

‘Was she dressed at this point?’

‘No,’ said Eric, ‘she was semi-naked, she hadn’t put on the clothes I’d found for her.’

‘And what happened next?’

‘She stumbled against me, and I took hold of her to stop her falling, then she kissed me fiercely.’

Eric affected to be distressed at this point and looked crumpled and wretched.

‘Then what happened?’ said Counsel.

‘We both fell to the floor, and in the heat of the moment, we had intercourse.’

‘I see,’ said Counsel. ‘What happened afterwards?’

‘About an hour later, I drove her home, but before we got there, she screamed at me to stop the car and disappeared into a cul-de-sac.’

‘Then what’?

‘I waited about five minutes but became concerned and went looking for her, but she had vanished, so I returned home. In the evening she phoned to tell me she'd gone home and changed her clothes and then gone back to work. She said she would see me in the office on the following day.'

'And did you speak when you saw her?' asked the Counsel.

'Yes,' said Eric, 'I said that she was a bitch and that she and Gilbert deserved each other.'

'How did she respond to that?'

'She told me to eff off, and said she hoped she would have her day in court and destroy my reputation. But I told her that I would tell the truth and my self-esteem would still be intact, whatever she tried to do to my reputation.'

'Did you then leave her office?'

'Yes. As I closed the door behind me, I heard her scream as if in anger, and the sound of something being thrown at the door.'

At the break for lunch, Sam told him how delighted she was by how Eric had kept his cool, she was tremendously impressed, and she felt the jury was convinced that he was speaking the truth.

*

It was Anna's turn in the dock in the afternoon. Eric actually felt briefly sorry for her, she seemed so distraught and looked haggard. Her hair was unwashed, and her makeup not applied.

When she was cross-examined by the defending solicitor, Anna's answers did not seem very coherent, and the judge asked her to speak up. She frequently shook her head as though she didn't understand the question and got totally confused over dates and times. Privately, Eric thought she was drugged but didn't voice his opinion. Her Counsel asked if she wanted an adjournment but again, she shook her head.

Later, after cross examination by the prosecuting Counsel, she lost her way completely and the judge called a recess. The evidence put before the court was so indictable that Anna's defence collapsed. When the court resumed just a few minutes later, the judge asked for the jury's verdict. All twelve found her guilty of manslaughter.

To Eric this was a great relief, but he was stunned when Anna was sentenced to five years in prison.

Chapter 30

After the court case, they adjourned to the 5-star hotel that Sam had booked for two nights, and invited Brian to join them for drinks in the bar to thank him for his constant positivity.

Sam's aim was to help Eric decide whether he felt committed to helping the company to survive, and if so, to spend a couple of days contacting various groups of people with a view to raising capital. He would also need to gain a commitment from the unions to work for the benefit of all interested parties.

'To us,' said Sam, raising her flute of champagne, her eyes flashing with pure joy. 'You did a masterly job of convincing the jury of your integrity.'

'I had total confidence in you,' said Brian,

'Thank you,' Eric said, 'but I'm stunned at the sentence. Still, justice had to be done.'

Sam was more forthright. 'Anna has no conscience. She showed no remorse for that poor cyclist and his family. Did you see them in court?' Eric confessed that he was so nervous and overwhelmed that he couldn't focus on anybody, not even the jury, and was totally surprised at Anna's performance. Eric decided that if Sam could accept his version of events, prior to their relationship developing, he could forgive himself and move on.

A dark cloud had lifted, and he felt released from the trauma of his courtroom experience. Sam refilled his glass. 'This is the first day of the rest of our lives.'

*

Later in the week, a rumour circulated in the office that Gilbert had gone to his wife's home town and begged for a reconciliation. Anna's poor defence in court was no doubt the result. Eric surmised that if Gilbert and his wife did get together again, then he would most likely want to move all his operations to the States.

Chapter 31

Sam suggested a holiday in South Africa, it might help to clear Eric's mind of the Anna affair. They also discussed moving away together as Eric knew that a complete break from the past was what he desperately needed. Sam was sympathetic, although she was still committed to saving the factory for its loyal employees.

The economic climate in the UK and Gilbert's moving to the States would be a big factor in whether Stallen Engineering was financially viable. Sam had contacted her business associates, and the feeling among them was that if Gilbert tried to resurrect her father's cutting tool and patent and market it, then a court action would be easier to bring under American law than trying to fight him in Britain.

Eric had found living with Sam had turned his life around. She was organised and intuitive, she gave out an aura of calm which Eric had sorely missed after Gloria's death. They both liked to cook, and shared various tastes and recipes, and enjoyed intimate dinner parties with Eric's friends from the golf club and the schoolfriends Sam had kept close ties with after her schooling in England.

They spent time visiting business colleagues whom Eric felt were in tune with the business ethics he espoused when dealing with other companies. Decisions would be made, and Eric felt capable of keeping his integrity intact. He developed connections with people who would help him to maintain good relationships with the movers and shakers in the twenty-first century and contribute to the survival and success of Stallen Engineering.

His past life and the negative memories associated with it seemed a million miles away. The only redeeming feature was the happiness of his marriage to Gloria and her indomitable spirit which Eric would cherish forever. Sam was his reward for keeping true to his values even under the greatest provocation from unscrupulous people. He was determined that Sam would be totally loved and cherished in return for her incredible feminine intuition and charisma which had brought him through a crisis.

www.ingramcontent.com/pod-product-compliance
Ingram Content Group UK Ltd.
Pitfield, Milton Keynes, MK11 3LW, UK
UKHW041959190726
13854UKWH00005B/2060